A Notchmas Carol

An unofficial Minecraft holiday story
inspired by Charles Dickens'
A Christmas Carol

By,

Published by Eclectic Esquire Media, LLC
P.O. Box 235094
Encinitas, CA 92023-5094

Inquiries and Information: *drblockbooks@gmail.com*

Table of Contents

Chapter One

The village of Squaresville was like most other villages in the land of Minecraft. It had many houses and shops. Villagers walked its streets during the day and stayed inside at night when the zombies roamed free. Players visited from time to time in order to make trades. Some villagers prospered by their trades while others gave away too much.

One of the greatest traders who had ever lived in Squaresville – or in any other Minecraft village – was named Ebenezer Scrooge.

I know what you are thinking: "What sort of a name is that?"

Well, it is an old name and Ebenezer was an old man, a *very* old man. He had lived for many years and had amassed a fortune in emeralds and diamonds the likes of which had never been seen or heard of in Squaresville or in any other village in all of Minecraft.

He was legendary for his wealth.

But, he was also legendary for his stinginess and cheapness. You see, Ebenezer believed that the best way to become wealthy was never to spend any money.

"If you don't buy anything," he would say with a snort, "you can never waste money. And wasting money is the worst thing in the world that a villager can do."

And so, Ebenezer made it his life's work to rip-off players and other villagers with trades so he would gain great wealth. He would loan emeralds to his fellow villagers at excessive interest rates. So, if he lent them 5 emeralds, they would have to pay him back with 10.

Ebenezer had so many trades and loans going on at any one time, he had to hire an assistant to help him keep track of everything. The assistant's name was Bob Cratchit.

I know what you are thinking again: "Bob is a pretty normal name, but Cratchit? What sort of name is that?"

It may surprise you that the name "Cratchit" is actually very common in some parts of the world. But, this is not a story about names. It is a story about Notchmas, the most important of all the holidays in Minecraft.

You see, today was the day before Notchmas. Also known as "Notchmas Eve."

Bob Cratchit was anxious to finish his work at Ebenezer Scrooge's office and return home to celebrate with his family.

"Mr. Scrooge?" asked Bob. "Is there any chance I can leave work a little early today?"

Scrooge looked up from his account books and cast a beady, suspicious, and disdainful eye in Bob's direction.

"Do I pay you to leave work early?" he said angrily.

Bob cast his eyes toward the floor. "No, sir, it is just that tomorrow is Notchmas, and I was hoping to spend some extra time with my family."

Scrooge clucked his tongue. "Notchmas? Already? Bah humbug! Isn't it enough that you get all day tomorrow off from work? Trying to extend Notchmas into a two-day spectacle is unacceptable and disgusting!"

"But sir," Bob continued, "Notchmas is when we celebrate the birth of our great creator, Notch. It is a time of peace and joy. What is wrong with celebrating it a little longer?"

"Enough!" yelled Scrooge. "You still have two more hours on your shift, and I expect you to work them in their entirety."

Bob nodded sadly. "Well, then, sir, could I put another piece of wood in the furnace? It is getting very cold and my hands are turning blue."

"Then rub your hands together. I cannot afford to let you burn forests of wood."

Bob sighed and returned to his work. He picked up the tiny nub of a pencil he used to write entries in the accounting ledger. Scrooge would not let him get a new pencil until the one he was using was smaller than a baby villager's pinky finger.

In between writing numbers and rubbing his hands, Bob looked out the window. There was a light dusting of snow on the ground. Bob smiled and thought, *Looks like it will be a white Notchmas.*

Now seems like a good time to explain some more details about Notchmas to those of you who may be unfamiliar with it.

As already mentioned in the story, Notchmas is believed to be the date on which Notch, the great creator of the world of Minecraft, was born.

Everyone in the Minecraft world — and I mean everyone: NPCs, passive mobs, hostile mobs, and even some players — celebrates Notchmas. It is the one day when no one fights or kills. No one trades. The only thing to be done is to be thankful for Notch the Creator and to eat lots and lots of food.

That is what Bob had planned. He and his family of Cratchits were going to sit around the table and eat mountains of cookies, cakes, chickens, carrots, soups and whatever else they might think of. They would sing songs and dance. They would tell stories and jokes and gave thanks to Notch.

Scrooge, on the other hand, hated Notchmas.

To him, it was the worst day of the year. It was the one day when he was forbidden from trading and therefore he was forbidden from earning money. Notchmas was, to Scrooge's thinking, the one day of the year where is *lost* money.

Oh, he knew it was a pretty awesome and dominant thing that Notch created the world of Minecraft and all that, but that was ancient history.

What is the point, thought Scrooge, *of making such a fuss about Notch and about wanting to spend a day with your family?*

Now you know all about Notchmas and what Bob and Scrooge thought about it. So, it should be no surprise to you that as Bob continued to make entries in the account book, he pondered how wonderful tomorrow would be.

And, soon enough, the bell in the office chimed six o'clock.

Bob put his pencil down and jumped up from his chair. Scrooge looked at him with a disdainful glance.

"Well, Mr. Scrooge, Merry Notchmas," said Bob.

"Bah humbug," responded Scrooge dismissively.

Bob stood there.

"What?" asked Scrooge.

Bob moved his foot nervously back and forth. "Is there any chance I could have a Notchmas bonus?"

Scrooge looked like he might have a heart attack and fall down dead right there. "A bonus? Do I not already pay you for your work?"

"Yes, but it's just that other employers –"

"I don't care what other stupid and ridiculous and *poor* employers do."

"But, the money would help with my son, Tim, he –"

Scrooge held up a hand. "Cratchit. Your family problems are not my concern. Go home and do your Notchmas-ing and then get back to work bright and early the day after Notchmas."

Bob sighed and walked to the door. As he pushed the door open, he said, "Merry Notchmas, anyway, Mr. Scrooge. Merry Notchmas."

Chapter Two

Scrooge shook his head as he watched the door close behind Cratchit. Scrooge felt sorry for Cratchit and other younger villagers. All they wanted to do was party and not work.

"The world is doomed," said Scrooge aloud, though he was alone. He was always alone, except when Cratchit was at work. Scrooge had no friends or family. He never thought about it, though, because all he ever thought about was money.

Many years ago, Scrooge had a business partner named Jacob Marley. (If you have any thoughts about this name, keep them to yourself.) Scrooge had liked Jacob. They both believed in working as much as possible and making as much money as possible.

Scrooge sighed at the warm and fuzzy memory as he continued reviewing his ledger books. He felt a warmth in his belly as he realized that he had made more money this month than he had in several years.

"Notchmas is good for business, at least," he said aloud again. "Everyone borrows to pay for their gifts and their feasts and their nonsense and then has to pay for them all year long."

And with that happy thought in his head, Scrooge stood up, took his scarf from the hook on which he had placed it early that morning, and wrapped it around his neck. He turned off the furnace and put out the torchlight. He walked to the office door, opened it, and, locking the door behind him, he stepped out into the night.

You are probably thinking what an idiot Scrooge is for walking through the village streets at night. What about the zombies and skeletons and spiders?

Well, even though he was an old man, Scrooge was so mean and nasty that even the hostile mobs normally avoided him. And, anyway, his house was next door to his office, so he only had to walk about five steps to get home.

But, tonight, there was a zombie standing near Scrooge's front door. Scrooge walked right up to the zombie and smacked it as hard as he could with a shovel he had pulled from his inventory.

"Ouch," moaned the zombie, rubbing its head.

Scrooge hit it again and it flashed red.

The zombie quickly moved out of attack range. "Don't you know it is Notchmas Eve, old man?" asked the zombie.

"And what of it, you pile of rotting stink?"

"We are supposed to live in harmony on Notchmas, so why not leave me alone for tonight?"

Scrooge grunted. "You too? If Notchmas Eve is the same as Notchmas, then why not just have Notchmas be every day of the year? We could all stop working, live in peace and sing *Kum Ba Yah* every day. Bah humbug!"

And with that, Scrooge unlocked the door to his house and stepped inside. The zombie just stared at the door and shook his head.

Scrooge sat down at his table and ate a dinner of cold chicken. He could make a single chicken last an entire week, so he only needed to have 52 chickens per year. This, he had calculated, *saved* him more money in a single year than many villagers *earned* in a year.

But, it also made him the most boring villager in the history of the universe because he ate the same food every day.

Can you imagine? Eating the same food everyday for an entire year?

It would be the most horrible thing ever. But, at least it was chicken and not mushroom stew every night. Talk about horrific!

And so, Scrooge finished his meal, checked the locks on his door and windows, and then prepared himself for bed.

As Scrooge tucked himself into bed, he read for a few minutes. It was a book about how to turn cobblestone into diamonds by using alchemy.

Scrooge didn't really believe alchemy was possible, but he had read just about every book ever written on the subject in case there might be some truth to the claims of alchemists who said they could turn rocks into precious minerals. At the very least, reading these books immediately before sleep filled his dreams with happy thoughts.

And then, Scrooge drifted off to sleep.

Chapter Three

Scrooge awoke in the middle of the pitch black night to the sound of clanging and dragging. He thought at first that it was coming from outside his bedroom window.

"Stupid zombies," he muttered, turning over in bed to get comfortable. "Always causing a ruckus in the middle of the night."

But then, he heard the sound again and realized that it was coming from *inside* of his house! He wondered if maybe a zombie had somehow broken into his house.

Very quietly, Scrooge got out of bed and walked to the large chest in the corner of his bedroom. He opened it and removed a diamond sword from his inventory. Scrooge was so old that he could barely lift the sword.

"I guess I will get my money's worth from you tonight," he

whispered to the sword in a nervous voice.

You may have noticed by now that Scrooge speaks aloud to himself a lot. This is what people do when they have alienated everyone and no one wants to be around them: they talk to themselves. It is a bit crazy, but they think it is normal. It is really quite sad.

The clanging and dragging was coming closer to Scrooge's bedroom door. In fact, he could now hear shambling footsteps as the noisy creature came closer and closer.

"I am ready for you zombie!" shouted Scrooge in an attempt to feel more courageous.

But, the truth was he had never been cornered by a zombie. The one time he had ever felt that his life was in danger, was when he was a young boy. Then, he simply ran away from the zombie and a player named Steve appeared out of nowhere and dispatched the zombie with a few quick blows from his sword.

"Eb-en-ez-er," moaned a voice from just outside the bedroom.

Scrooge was startled. "How ... how do you know my name, zombie?"

"Eb-en-ez-er," it moaned again.

"Stay back foul being," Scrooge demanded with a shaky voice as he held his sword in front of him.

And, then, the creature stepped through the door and Scrooge could see that it was not a zombie after all.

Well, not proper zombie anyway.

It looked more like a zombie villager, but even that was not right. It was true that the creature appeared to be a villager who appeared to have died a long time ago, his flesh was rotting after all. But, there was no smell of decay. In fact, the villager was translucent, like a ghost.

"Ebenezer, it is I, Jacob," said the hideous creature.

In shock, Scrooge saw now that the clanging and dragging noises had been made by a long, heavy iron chain wrapped around the creature which dragged behind it.

Scrooge was nearly dumb-struck. "Ja ... Ja ... Jacob? Jacob Marley? My old business partner?"

"The very same," moaned the spirit, a look of agony passing across his face.

"But, how are you here? You died five years ago," said Scrooge with a hushed voice.

The spirit moaned a horrible moan from the depths of its soul but spoke no words. The sound frightened Scrooge so much that he dropped his sword.

Recovering from his fright, Scrooge asked, "What has happened to you, Jacob?"

"I have been punished for the greed and selfishness of my life. Just as you will be punished in the afterlife if you do not change."

Scrooge swallowed hard. "Surely, Jacob, you have not been punished because of your ... because of *our* successful business?"

"It was the price of success that has led to my punishment," said Jacob. "I ignored my family, I ignored my village, and I ignored the most important thing of all, Notchmas."

Scrooge shivered with fear. "But, how are you punished in the afterlife? I thought you would just respawn in another village. This makes no sense."

"Sense it need not make," said Jacob. "Notch demands that his creations follow his rules and celebrate his creation. Failure to do that will result in a suspension of re-spawn privileges."

All of the color drained from Scrooge's face. "No respawn

privileges? So, where do you reside now?"

"In the deepest, darkest corner of the Nether. No player or NPC ever goes there, not even Herobrine. I spend my days dragging this chain and cursing my life."

Scrooge reached out to Jacob to lay a comforting hand on his arm, but Scrooge's hand passed through Jacob's shape as if nothing were there. The only sensation Scrooge felt was one of icy death.

As he pulled his hand back, Scrooge asked, "Why have you

appeared to me now, after so many years?"

At this question, Jacob pointed at Scrooge, extending the bony block of his ghostly hand, from which most of the flesh had fallen, and said simply, "I have come to teach you a lesson. If you learn, we may both be saved. If you do not learn, you will suffer my fate."

"No!" screamed Scrooge.

"Yes," muttered Jacob.

"Then, please, old friend, teach me the lesson."

Jacob shook his head slowly. "I am not the teacher."

"Then who?" asked Scrooge, not sure he really wanted to know the answer.

"You will be visited this night by three creatures who will show you all you need to know to learn your lesson. Pay attention and ... well ... don't be a jerk."

Scrooge nodded his head quickly. "I understand. I understand."

"Good-bye, Ebenezer," said Jacob as he vanished from sight.

Scrooge stood there for a moment, staring at the spot where Jacob and his heavy chains had been only a second ago.

"Was that real?" Scrooge asked aloud. "Could I have been visited by the ghost of my dead business partner?"

Scrooge inspected the wooden floor of the bedroom for marks, for surely the heavy chains dragged by Jacob would have left scratches on the floor. There was nothing.

"Maybe that chicken I had for dinner was rotten. And this was all an illusion caused by indigestion?" suggested Scrooge to himself.

Scrooge leaned his diamond sword against the wall next to his bed and got back under his covers.

"Yes, that is it. My dinner has upset my stomach and given me bad dreams. Jacob is dead and buried, not Notch's messenger from the afterlife. It is impossible."

Satisfied with his explanation to himself, Scrooge made himself comfortable and quickly fell asleep.

Chapter Four

Scrooge's eyes were still closed when he noticed flickering light filtering through his eyelids.

"Did I leave a torch on?" he mumbled as he opened his eyes.

But, it was no torch. It was far too bright for that. For there, standing – or should I say hovering – at the end of his bed was a bright, burning blaze!

"What are you doing here?" asked Scrooge in terror, pulling his blanket to his chin in a feeble attempt to protect himself.

The blaze said nothing.

Scrooge could not believe what he asked the blaze next, but he asked anyway because, after all, how often do you find a blaze hovering in your bedroom? He asked, "Are you one of the creatures Jacob sent to visit me?"

The blaze nodded its head to indicate the answer was "yes."

"So, what do I do?"

The blaze extended a flame and moved it toward itself, as if beckoning Scrooge to follow it.

"You want me to follow you?"

The blaze nodded.

Scrooge got out of bed and stood up. "Where are we going?"

The blaze continued his silent treatment of Scrooge, but suddenly Scrooge felt as if they were flying. Scrooge looked down and confirmed it.

Scrooge screamed with fright, "How is this possible? How can we be flying over the village?"

The blaze said nothing. Scrooge said nothing more. All

he could do was hope that the blaze did not drop him to the ground, for surely he would die.

And suddenly, as quickly as it had started, Scrooge and the blaze were on the ground in another portion of the village.

Scrooge regained his composure and looked around.

"I know this place," he said to the blaze. "I have been here before."

Scrooge noticed a small fence, some planted crops, and a barn in the distance. The pleasant glow of torchlight was coming from inside the barn. Then he knew.

"This is Old Feziwig's farm!" he exclaimed. (I know what you are thinking. Feziwig? But, hey, these are old-timey villager names, so bear with me.)

The blaze nodded to indicate that Scrooge was correct.

"But," said Scrooge with concern, "Feziwig's farm burned to the ground forty years ago during the great zombie invasion. How can this be his farm?"

The blaze once again beckoned Scrooge to follow it.

The two quietly approached the barn from which the glowing light came. As they drew nearer, Scrooge could hear live music coming from the barn and could smell the delightful smell of cookies, cakes, roasting chickens and sizzling steaks.

As he looked into the barn, he realized what he was seeing. It was a Notchmas celebration from when he was a 12-year old villager!

"How is this possible, blaze, that I can be present at something that happened when I was a boy?"

The blaze shrugged its fiery shoulders and pointed at the party, as if instructing Scrooge to watch.

Scrooge did watch and saw himself as a boy speaking with one of his friends from back in the day, Matthew.

"Matt, cool Notchmas feast, isn't it?" asked young Scrooge.

"So totally cool. It was nice of Feziwig to invite our families to his house for the feast," said Matt. "He sure is a generous man."

Old Scrooge realized his parents would be there in this …

this .... What was this anyway? A memory?

He looked around and saw his mother and father eating cookies and laughing with Feziwig.

Scrooge realized that he had not thought about his parents in years, maybe decades. He sighed at the memory of them.

Scrooge's parents had been poor farmers with a plot of land on the edge of the village of Squaresville. They never had many emeralds because almost no one traded with them. Scrooge had been very poor as a boy, but he realized at that moment that in spite of his poverty he had never been unhappy.

As Scrooge wiped a tear from his eye, he looked back at his younger self and Matt.

Young Scrooge chomped on a cookie and asked with his mouth full, "Do you think you'll get any Notchmas presents?"

Matt shrugged. "Maybe. I usually get some sticks or rocks to craft with. But, I am hoping to get a bow and a few arrows so I can start hunting bunnies for food. What about you?"

"I probably won't get anything," said young Scrooge sadly. "I wish I could get an emerald all my own. I love how they sparkle."

"Yeah," said Matt, stuffing a piece of cake into his mouth. "Emeralds are cool, but if you can hunt, you can trade for emeralds. If I get a bow, I'll teach you to hunt."

"Cool," said young Scrooge. "I wish we could go off and be explorers like the players that pass through town. I'd love to see all the biomes of the world and maybe even the End or the Nether."

Matt laughed. "Yeah, right, we are just sons of poor farmers. We'll never get out of this village."

Young Scrooge suddenly got angry. "I am totally getting out of this village when I get older. I vow to explore the world!"

"Chill, dude," said Matt. "Fine, go explore the world. See if I care."

"Fine, I will," said young Scrooge with finality.

Matt sighed. "Let's stop arguing and eat."

Young Scrooge let the anger drain from his face and the two young villagers ran back to the table of food and ate their fill and then some.

Old Scrooge had watched the exchange with a smile, until he realized that he had never fulfilled his vow to explore the world. Yes, he was wealthy beyond the dreams of any other villagers, but he had given up his childhood dream in order to become rich.

Scrooge looked at the blaze with sad, watery eyes and sniffed. "Oh, creature, you have awakened an ancient memory that has saddened me. Have you shown me all that you need to show me? I wish to return home from this Notchmas past."

And then, without any warning, Scrooge found himself back in his bed. The blaze was gone. He was alone.

Scrooge sat in his bed. He was in shock.

"Was this just another dream caused by indigestion, or did that blaze really transport me through time to a Notchmas of my childhood?"

There was no one there to answer his question, and Scrooge slumped down under his covers and, to his surprise, soon fell asleep again.

Chapter Five

Scrooge felt like he had barely fallen back to sleep when he heard a clicking sound in his room.

By now, he knew not to wonder aloud at what the sound might be. Instead, he ignited the torch by his bedside and looked into the shadows of his room.

Scrooge knew, of course, that he was going to see something

strange and mysterious, maybe even a little scary. But, he was not prepared for what he saw floating before him.

A wither!

Scrooge pulled his blanket up to his chin and muttered, "Did … did Jacob send you?"

The central head of the three-headed wither nodded to indicate "yes." The two side heads simply stared directly into Scrooge's eyes.

It was terrifying.

"What do you want me to do?" asked Scrooge.

The right-side head suddenly jerked to the side, indicating that Scrooge should get out of bed.

"You don't speak either?" asked Scrooge.

The left-side head shook side-to-side, indicating "no."

"Seriously?" said Scrooge with exasperation. "It would be a lot easier for me to learn my lessons if you creatures would speak instead of gesture."

The wither did not like being reprimanded by so weak a creature as an old villager. The main wither head opened its mouth and shot a skull out, hitting Scrooge.

Scrooge suddenly felt very sick, as if all the blood in his body had turned to ice. He felt dizzy and nauseous and began to stumble around. Scrooge collapsed to the ground, twitching as the wither hovered above him, all three of its heads scowling at him.

But then, just as suddenly as the wither effect had harmed him, it was gone.

Scrooge stood up, gasping for breath. He was amazed – truly, honestly amazed – that he was still alive.

"I apologize," he said sincerely. "Lead and I shall follow."

Scrooge then felt an invisible force encircle his waist and lift him from the ground.

"Ugh, again with the flying," muttered Scrooge.

The wither and Scrooge flew above the village, but unlike his previous flight with the blaze, this was a short flight, lasting mere seconds.

When they were back on the ground, the right-side head of

the wither nodded in the direction of a house.

"Shall I go inside?" asked Scrooge.

The central wither head shook side-to-side. The wither floated to a window and peered inside.

"I should look through the window then?"

The central head nodded.

Scrooge cautiously looked around. "I know we are in my village, but I do not recognize this house. Where have you taken me, wither?"

The wither wordlessly stood aside from the window.

When Scrooge looked inside, he was surprised to see his employee, Bob Cratchit, and his family sitting down for a Notchmas feast. And, by some magic employed by the wither, Scrooge could hear what they were saying.

"Bob," said a woman who must have been his wife, "I can't believe Mr. Scrooge is so cheap and heartless that he did not give you a Notchmas bonus."

"Now, now, Emily, Mr. Scrooge has been my employer

for many years and my job has allowed us to build this home and feed our family."

Scrooge smiled and muttered, "Loyal Cratchit."

"But," continued Bob, "we certainly could have a much nicer home if he were a more generous man."

Scrooge turned his smile upside down. "Humbug."

Emily Cratchit sighed. "Enough talk of that vile man. Let us enjoy our Notchmas feast."

Scrooge did not like Emily Cratchit. He turned to the

wither. "Is this the present year Notchmas? No time travel?"

All three heads of the wither nodded simultaneously.

So, thought Scrooge, *this creature is showing me the Notchmas present.*

In addition to Cratchit's wife, Scrooge noticed that Bob had six children, three daughters and three sons.

"By Notch's beard, he has quite a brood. He told me he had children, but six! I had no idea."

Scrooge watched as the family ate and sang and exchanged gifts. It was all very pleasant, but Scrooge could not understand what he was supposed to learn from this visitation.

When Scrooge was about to ask the wither to take him home, Scrooge saw the youngest boy, "Tiny Tim" they had been calling him, get up from the table.

Scrooge saw that he walked with a crutch and Tim's right leg looked hideous. It seemed as if it should have been attached to a zombie, not a 6 year old villager.

"What is wrong with the child?" Scrooge asked the wither, who, of course, said nothing.

Scrooge continued to watch as the children cleared the table. Bob brought out a drum and played a song. The family sang. Then, the children went to bed.

Scrooge felt like a freak, staring in the window at the Cratchit house all night long, but the wither would not let him leave. So, he continued to stare. It was then that he saw what the wither wanted him to see.

Emily approached Bob and hugged him.

"We need more money for Tim," she said sobbing.

Bob nodded.

"The only one who can cure him is that witch who lives far from here. The journey and the cure will cost at least 500 emeralds," continued Emily. "How can we get the money?"

"Maybe I can ask Mr. Scrooge for a loan?" suggested Bob.

Emily laughed. "That ghoul? He'd just as soon sell his mother for 2 emeralds than loan you anything."

Scrooge stiffened at the insult.

"I still have to try," said Bob. "Without the cure, Tim will die."

Scrooge gasped. "Is that true, wither? Will Tiny Tim die?"

The wither nodded.

Emily spoke through sobs, "I can't believe that zombie gave him the zombie touch. If only I hadn't let him play outside that one evening, he would be a normal boy. Now, he is slowly changing into a zombie villager!"

"No," said Scrooge to the wither. "Not the zombie touch."

And with that, Scrooge found himself back in bed, and the wither nowhere to be seen.

Chapter Six

Scrooge did not go to sleep again. He knew there was a third creature yet to visit him, and he just assumed stay awake. If he was dreaming all this, he would not have another visitor. If it was real, then there was no point in sleeping.

Well, let me tell you, it *was* real. Very, very real. And, if it hadn't been real until now, it just *got* real.

His third visitor was even more terrifying than the wither, if you can believe it. And, you will.

His third visitor was Herobrine himself!

"He ... He ... Herobrine?" Scrooge asked through teeth chattering with fear.

And, to Scrooge's surprise and unlike his previous visitors, Herobrine spoke, "The one and only."

"Are you here to kill me?"

Herobrine laughed heartily. "Kill you? On Notchmas Eve? No way."

"You celebrate Notchmas?" asked Scrooge in shock. "I thought you were Notch's enemy."

Herobrine shook his head. "Notch has no enemies or friends. He is the Creator. He is above and beyond us all. Above and beyond our comprehension. I, like you, must honor him on Notchmas."

"Bah humbug," said Scrooge. "Why must I stop making money for a pointless holiday?" Scrooge seriously surprised himself that he would be so brave in front of Herobrine.

Herobrine's eyes glowed red with anger. He leaned forward and seemed to double in size as he spoke loudly, "Have you learned nothing, you fool?"

Scrooge began to tremble in his bed. "What do you mean?"

"Did you not see yourself as a boy?"

"Yes."

"Did you not see Tiny Tim?"

"Yes."

"Well...?" asked Herobrine expectantly.

"I still don't see how those visions are supposed to teach me something that will help me escape Jacob's fate," said Scrooge, adding, "If that really was Jacob."

"Oh, it was Jacob alright," said Herobrine. "Look, I think you are a hopeless, pathetic kook, but Jacob has asked me to show you one more thing before he gives up on you. Are you ready?"

Scrooge got out of bed and stood before Herobrine, trembling. Herobrine was tall and strong, full of vitality. This was a great contrast to Scrooge's weak and shriveled body. Suddenly, Scrooge felt ashamed for never exercising, for never taking walks, for never exploring the world.

As Scrooge slowly went down the rabbit hole of self-loathing, Herorbine snapped his fingers.

The two were instantly transported to a familiar location.

"Why," said Scrooge, "we are standing in front of the door to my house."

"Yes, we are, only it is five years into the future on Notchmas."

Scrooge rolled his eyes. "Jacob wanted you to show me my front door on a Notchmas future? Kinda stupid, am I right?"

Herobrine slapped his head. "Just watch."

Scrooge stood there for a moment. He saw some villagers come around a corner and begin walking in front of him and Herobrine, oblivious to their presence. He recognized the villagers but could not remember their names.

At the same moment, he – his future self, actually – emerged from the office next door and began the short walk to his house.

And, just as Scrooge passed the group of villagers, he suddenly clutched his chest, fell forward, and died, leaving only a few sparkles of light, glowing like snowflakes in the night.

Scrooge gasped and asked, "You have come to show me my death?"

"Keep watching," instructed Herobrine.

The group of villagers had stopped walking. They were now staring at the despawn point and last resting place of Ebenezer Scrooge.

"It's about time that evil geezer died," said one of them.

"May Notch curse his soul," said another.

"May he never respawn," said a third.

As they walked away, one of them kicked the ground where Scrooge had died and whispered,

"Serves you right for ignoring them."

Scrooge had observed the scene in shock. He knew that he was not well-liked in his village – the rich never are – but he had no idea he was actually hated. So hated, in fact, that his fellow villagers would want his soul to be cursed by Notch.

Scrooge looked at Herobrine with questioning eyes, and asked, "How can I avoid this fate?"

"You cannot avoid death."

"No, I mean Jacob's fate. How can I avoid an eternity of torment in the Nether?"

Herobrine looked at Scrooge and there was a sadness in his glowing eyes. "I am not allowed to tell you. Every villager has free will as a gift from Notch. You must find the answer yourself."

And then, for the first time since he was a very young boy, Scrooge began to sob. And his sobs soon became a strong cry. And, eventually, he was wailing with a frustrated agony.

He stood there, a river of anguished tears running down his face.

He felt utterly alone.

And then, Herobrine snapped his fingers.

Chapter Seven

Scrooge's next memory was waking up in bed early on Notchmas morning.

If this had been a normal Notchmas, Scrooge would have eaten a breakfast cookie, paced around his house all day in anger because he could not work, and then he would have eaten some chicken and gone to bed.

But today, he was filled with energy and purpose. Whether his visitors had been real or only the figment of his imagination, he did not care. The visits had changed him.

Scrooge got dressed in his finest and most festive suit. He thought he looked wonderful, though the suit was out of fashion by thirty years, so he looked more eccentric than stylish.

Scrooge stuffed several hundred emeralds into his inventory and then walked out his front door.

The streets had a light dusting of snow and there was a chill in the air. Scrooge could see inside numerous houses that families were enjoying their Notchmas breakfasts of cookies, cakes and other delicious sweet things.

But, Scrooge had spent enough time last night watching others. Today, he would act.

He strode purposefully to the butcher's house and banged on the door. The butcher came to the door and frowned when he saw it was Scrooge.

"I'll pay your loan back next week, Mr. Scrooge, I promise," said the butcher.

"Silence, man, I am not here about that. I am here to purchase ten of your finest chickens and two hams. How fast can you wrap them up?"

"Well, normally I don't work on Notchmas, but I guess I can make an exception for you."

In a few minutes, the butcher returned with several parcels filled with the requested items.

"That will be five emeralds," said the butcher.

"Here, take ten emeralds," said Scrooge.

The butcher was so surprised by Scrooge's unprecedented generosity, that he forgot to say thank you.

But, it was no matter, Scrooge had already tucked the food into his inventory and was rushing away to his next stop.

As Scrooge dashed through the village, the villagers stared at him with amazement and shouted, "What's your hurry, Mr. Scrooge?" and "Where's the fire?" and "Are you being chased by a creeper?" and "Watch it, buddy!"

Scrooge never broke his stride as he responded, "On my way to a Notchmas feast" and "I have no idea" and "No" and "Pardon me, madam!"

And so, it went on like this for the next few minutes as Scrooge ran as quickly as he could, which, because Scrooge was quite old, was really more of a trot than a run.

As he trotted, Scrooge passed by all the homes and businesses he had helped create by lending them emeralds. It was then that Scrooge realized he had been looking at his business the wrong way. He was not in business just to make emeralds and make himself rich, but he was in business to help others realize their dreams, and as a side-effect of that, he became rich.

At this thought, Scrooge's eyes began to tear up, and he wiped the water from them.

"Maybe I did learn something after all, Jacob," whispered Scrooge aloud.

It was then that Scrooge arrived at his destination: the Cratchit home.

It looked just as it had during last night's visitation. Since Scrooge had never bothered to visit Cratchits' house before, he decided that the wither really had taken him there last night because otherwise he could not have known what the house looked like.

Scrooge walked confidently to the front door and knocked hard with his old, blocky hand.

When Mrs. Cratchit opened the door, her face betrayed her shock, surprise, and disgust at seeing Scrooge on her doorstep.

"Mr. Scrooge?" she said. "What a ... um ... pleasant surprise."

Bob Cratchit joined his wife in the doorway. "Mr. Scrooge? Is there some emergency at the office? Isn't there some way I can stay home on Notchmas?"

Scrooge laughed. (Bob realized it was the first time he had ever heard Scrooge laugh a real laugh, not the choked snort he normally emitted.) "Bob, of course you can have Notchmas off. In fact, I stopped by to join your feast."

Emily Cratchit looked at her husband with a no-way-that-is-going-to-happen look. Bob got the hint.

"Well, uh, you see, Mr. Scrooge," began Bob, "Notchmas is our special family time and we like to keep it that way."

Scrooge was sad.

"Yes," said Mrs. Cratchit, "and we only have enough food for our family of eight."

Scrooge's face lit up. "Ah, but that is where you are wrong," he said as he pulled the chickens and hams from his inventory.

When the food came out, the six Cratchit children suddenly appeared behind their parents. Even Tiny Tim came as quickly as he could, hobbling toward the door on his zombie-infested leg and crutch.

The children had begun to drool at the sight of so much food. In fact, the fronts of their robes had small wet spots on them where the drool was collecting. They had never seen so much food in one place.

"Please, mother," said Tiny Tim, "let him stay. It is what Notch would do."

Mrs. Cratchit sighed. "I suppose you are right, Tim. And, well, it is a lot of food."

"Then it is settled," said Scrooge as he walked into the house and put the food on the table.

Scrooge then turned to Mr. and Mrs. Cratchit. "May I speak with you privately?"

As the children were occupied by arranging the food on the table, Bob and Emily directed Scrooge into the next room to speak.

"Bob," said Scrooge, "I've been a cruel boss to you."

"Oh, no sir, you haven't," said Bob, but Scrooge cut him off.

"No, it is true. I see that now. I make you work long hours for little pay. I keep you away from your family because I am a lonely, greedy villager. That is going to change."

Bob wanted to say something, but he was in shock.

Scrooge continued. "So, I want you to take the entire week off."

Bob was still in shock. His mouth was hanging open now. His wife's mouth was also hanging open, and she was beginning to cry.

"And, I am going to make you a partner in my business. You work as much or as little as you want and you will get a proportional share of the profits."

Bob was crying now too. He was on his knees kissing Scrooge's hand.

Scrooge pulled his hand away. "Get up, Bob! That is disgusting. Don't make me take back my offer."

"Sorry, Mr. Scrooge," said Bob, standing up. "It is just ...

well ... it is a Notchmas Miracle."

Scrooge shook his head. "No, it is just what is right. But, you know, I would like to offer you a real Notchmas Miracle."

"What more could you possibly offer us?" asked Mrs. Cratchit.

"This," said Scrooge as he pulled out a sack of 500 emeralds. "This to help you get Tim's leg cured."

At this point, both of the Crachits began crying uncontrollably with joy and relief and thanksgiving. They hugged

Scrooge and he did not push them away. It was the first time he had felt the loving contact of another villager since his mother died over forty years ago.

Scrooge too began to cry.

* * *

A few hours later, after they had eaten their fill of food and cookies and other Notchmas treats, the Cratchits, their six children, and Mr. Scrooge sat by the hearth enjoying the warmth of the fire.

It was then that Tiny Tim rose and hobbled over to Scrooge and stood next to him. Tim took Scrooge's hand in his and then he turned to look at his family.

And then, Tim spoke in his squeaky voice, "May Notch bless this house and everyone in it, including Mr. Scrooge."

A Notchmas Miracle, indeed, thought Scrooge.

It was then that Scrooge, nearly overcome with the emotion of the moment, looked out the window nearest to him.

He could not be certain, but he thought he saw a large,

square face with kind eyes and a beard looking back at him for the briefest of moments. He saw the face smile, and then vanish.

Notch?

The End

Please leave a review.

Thanks for reading *A Notchmas Carol*. I hope you liked it.

Could you spare a moment and leave a review where you bought it? It would really help me out and it will let me know what you think about the book.

You are awesome!

A Note from Dr. Block

I, Dr. Block, believe that Minecraft is the greatest game ever created, mainly because it has the most awesome characters and mobs ever created.

If you want to be alerted when I release a new book, be sure to **sign up for my email list** at *www.drblockbooks.com* or follow any of my social media platforms. I'm on Facebook, Twitter, and Instagram under @drblockbooks. I am also on Goodreads, just search for Dr. Block.

I recommend signing up for the newsletter because you will get **two free**, *subscriber-exclusive short stories* as well as a periodic newsletter.

Best wishes,
Dr. Block

Coloring Book

If you like to color, be sure to check out my unofficial Minecraft coloring book.

This coloring book contains **76 images**, including all current mobs as of version 1.17, as well as the Warden, Alex, and Steve. Check out the sample pages:

Also by Dr. Block

The Complete Baby Zeke: Books 1-9 (**also available in audiobook**)
The Complete Baby Zeke: Books 10-12 (**also available in audiobook**)

THE LIGHTNING TRILOGY
Baby Zeke: Diary of a Chicken Jockey, Book 13: A New Enemy
Baby Zeke: Diary of a Chicken Jockey, Book 14: Shadow Light
Baby Zeke: Diary of a Chicken Jockey, Book 15: Dark Fate

The Complete Baby Zeke: Books 13-15 (**also available in audiobook**)

Otis: Diary of a Baby Zombie Pigman, Book 1
Otis: Diary of a Baby Zombie Pigman, Book 2: Konichi Juan
Otis: Diary of a Baby Zombie Pigman, Book 3: Training

Creeptastic (**also available in audiobook**)

Diary of a Werewolf Steve, Books 1-3

Spooky Halloween Tales for Minecrafters

Diary of Herobrine: Origins
Diary of Herobrine: Prophecy
Diary of Herobrine: Apotheosis

Diary of a Minecraft Bat (**also available in audiobook**)

Diary of a Spider Chicken, Books 1-3

Diary of a Surfer Villager, Season One, Books 1-20
Diary of a Surfer Villager, Season Two, Books 21-30
Diary of a Surfer Villager, Season Three, *IN PROGRESS*

The Ballad of Winston the Wandering Trader, Books 1-5 (Season One)
The Ballad of Winston the Wandering Trader, Books 6-10 (Season Two)
The Ballad of Winston the Wandering Trader, Books 11-15 (Season Three; *IN PROGRESS*)

Tales of the Glitch Guardians, Book 1 – Origins
Tales of the Glitch Guardians, Book 2 – Kindred
Tales of the Glitch Guardians, Book 3 – Firestorm

The Ultimate Unofficial Mega Mob Mania **Coloring Book** for Minecrafters

With **Dave Villager:**
Dave the Villager and Surfer Villager: Crossover Crisis, Books 1 and 2

Made in United States
North Haven, CT
11 December 2021